For Sumana Seeboruth x – J.W.

For my mum, Elizabeth – R.C.

First published 2021 by Macmillan Children's Books
an imprint of Pan Macmillan
The Smithson, 6 Briset Street, London EC1M 5NR
EU representative: Macmillan Publishers Ireland Limited,
Mallard Lodge, Lansdowne Village, Dublin 4
Associated companies throughout the world.
www.panmacmillan.com

ISBN (PB): 978-1-5290-4314-3

Based on the original story *Alice's Adventures in Wonderland*,
written by Lewis Carroll and illustrated by Sir John Tenniel,
first published by Macmillan & Co. Ltd in 1865

1 3 5 7 9 8 6 4 2

A CIP catalogue record for this book is available from the British Library.

Printed in China

Alice's Adventures in WONDERLAND

Jeanne Willis & Ross Collins

MACMILLAN CHILDREN'S BOOKS

Once upon a golden day, beside a silver brook,
Alice and her older sister sat and read a book.
But the book was very boring – Alice shook her head,
'It hasn't any pictures! What's the use?' she said.

Alice made a daisy chain to help the time to pass,
when suddenly a talking rabbit
ran across the grass.

Looking at his pocket watch, he cried,
'I'm late, I'm late.'

Alice hurried after him –
'Wait, White Rabbit, wait!'

'Will my kitty miss me?' wondered Alice as she fell.

Down the winding rabbit hole, down the deepest well,

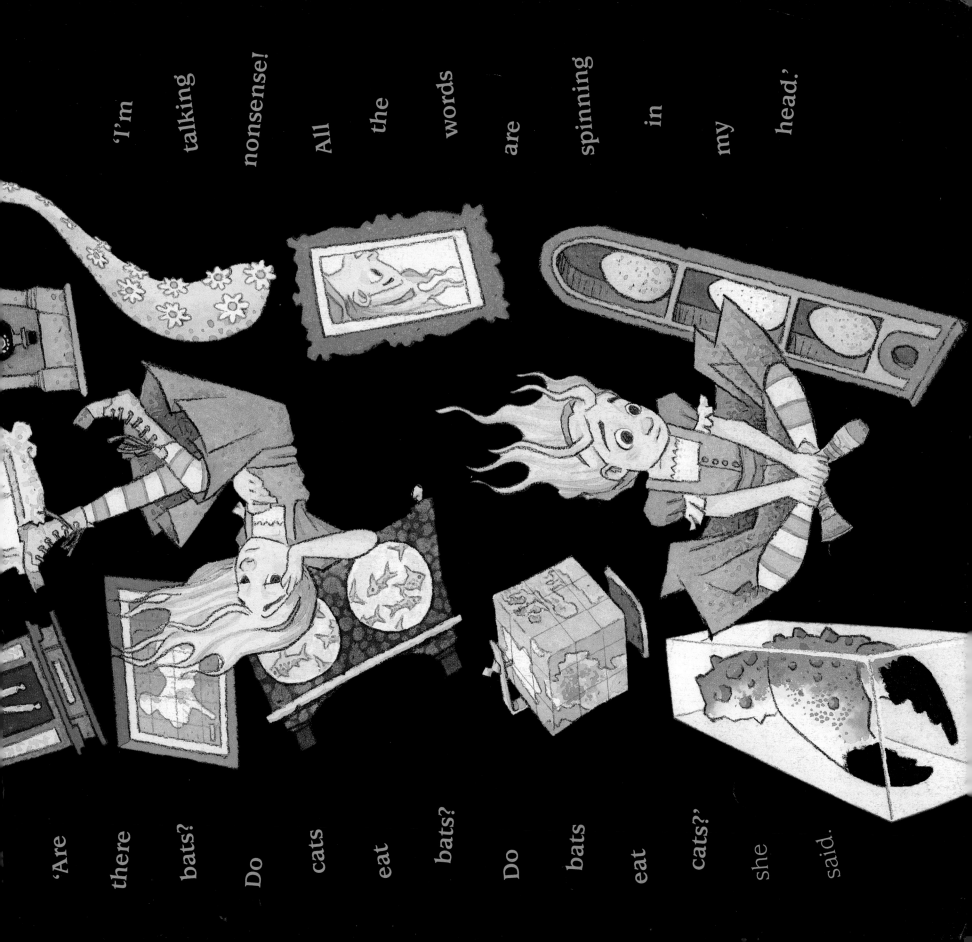

'I'm talking nonsense! All the words are spinning in my head.'

'Are there bats? Do cats eat *bats*? Do bats eat cats?' she said.

She landed with a bump
inside a hall with tiny doors.

The rabbit sped off muttering,
'My whiskers and my paws!'

She found a key and tried it in a door behind a curtain.
'If only I could shrink,' she said, 'I'd fit through it for certain!'

'I'm curious to know what's
in that bottle on the table.'
Alice pulled the cork out –
it said **'Drink Me!'** on the label.

She took a sip and shrunk!
But then she couldn't
reach the key.

'The table is too *tall*,' she sighed.
'There's not enough of me.'

She ate a piece of currant cake
and had the strangest feeling,
her body had begun
to grow . . .

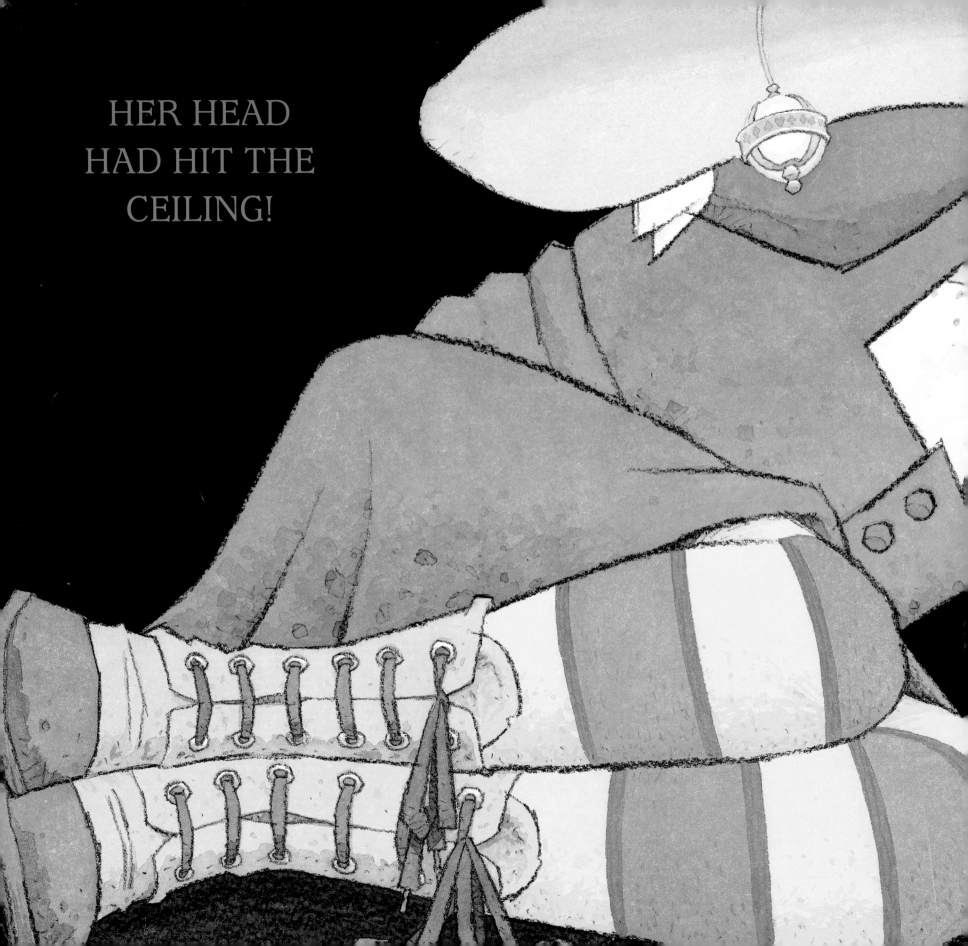

HER HEAD
HAD HIT THE
CEILING!

On the floor, she saw the rabbit's
white kid gloves and fan.
**'He dropped them! I will give
them back,'** said Alice, **'if I can.'**

'But I'm so tall,' she wept.
**'I could be stuck in here for years.
To pass the time, I'll use the fan
to waft away my tears.'**

The fan made Alice shrink and off she ran to Rabbit's house.
'I'm tired,' she said, **'of being not much taller than a mouse.'**

'Oh look! Another bottle! I will just drink half, no more . . .'
She grew too huge to fit the room, her feet were out the door.

Rabbit threw some pebbles and they all turned into cake.

'I'll eat them,' Alice said. 'To see
what difference they might make.'

She shrank, went through the
tiny door as quickly as she could,
and found a giant caterpillar
waiting in the wood.

'I'm far too small or tall!' she said.
'Whatever shall I do?'
'Eat my mushroom, child,' he said.
'It's very good for you.'

Alice chewed until she grew into
her normal size and . . .

In a tree, a Cheshire Cat appeared before her eyes.

'Go and see the Hatter now!' it said. 'He's having tea.

He's mad – but so is everyone, including you and me.'

The cat began to vanish from his tail-tip to his chin.
The only thing he left behind was his enormous grin.

Alice found the Hatter with a dormouse and a hare.
She asked to join the party but they didn't want to share.

'**No room!**' the Hatter bellowed.
'**My watch is broken, see?**
And as it's always six o'clock,
it's always time for tea.'

The Dormouse told a story
which no one could believe,
so they put him in the teapot –
and Alice had to leave!

She wandered down a garden path
beside a flower bed,
where the gardeners were painting
all the white roses red.
In marched the guards with the
King and Queen of Hearts.

'OFF WITH THEIR HEADS!'
she said, 'Before the croquet starts.'

The queen then turned to Alice and invited her to play with hedgehogs and flamingos in a strange game of croquet.

The flamingos flew away and all the hedgehogs went to bed.

The queen lost her temper and yelled,

'OFF WITH HER HEAD!'

When the trumpets sounded, she took Alice by the hand.
'The trial has begun!' she said. **'The prisoner's in the stand!'**
They both ran like the wind until they reached the Royal Court.

'Is that the Hatter eating bread and butter?'
Alice thought.

She sat beside the dormouse. **'You are squashing me, you know.'**
He groaned, and Alice had a feeling that she'd begun to grow.

'Who stole the tarts?' the judge demanded. **'Alice, was it you?'**
'You're talking nonsense,' she replied. **'Just like you always do.'**

'YOU'RE NOTHING BUT A PACK OF CARDS!' cried Alice in despair.

The pack rose up and all the cards went flying through the air.

They flapped and fluttered round her head and Alice gave a scream. And . . . .

She woke up on the grassy bank –
but was it just a dream?

Was the chatter of the Hatter
just the burble of the brook?
Were all the creatures that she met
just pictures in a book?

Or maybe there's a world
that only children understand . . .

And sometimes, just like Alice,
do you go to Wonderland?